Contents

Introduction

'Where do you think I've been these last eight years?' He looked quite pleased with himself. 'Prison. Malloy's the name. Moose Malloy. The Great Bend bank job – that was me. On my own, too. Forty thousand dollars.'

If anyone could rob a bank on his own, it's Moose Malloy. He's as hard as stone and as big as a bus. Now he's out of prison, and he wants two things: to know who gave his name to the police eight years ago, and to find his girlfriend.

Moose means trouble, and it's the sort of trouble a private detective should stay away from. So of course Philip Marlowe runs straight into it: trouble with the police, trouble with women, trouble with almost every criminal in California . . . And trouble with murder. Even when he tries to walk away from it, this sort of trouble just follows him around . . .

Raymond Chandler is one of the greatest modern detective writers. He turned the American crime story into a kind of art.

He was born in 1888 in Chicago, Illinois, but was brought up and educated in England. He worked as a reporter in London before returning, in 1912, to the USA. After fighting in France during World War I, he lived and worked in California. He lost his job in 1932. Then he started to write crime stories for magazines. His first book, *The Big Sleep* (1939), was about a private detective, Philip Marlowe. It was a great success, and he wrote about Marlowe in many other books, including *Farewell, My Lovely* (1940), *The High Window* (1942), *The Lady in the Lake* (1944) and *The Long Goodbye* (1953). Many of his books have been made into successful films.

Raymond Chandler died in 1959.

Chapter 1   Moose Malloy

It was a warm day, almost the end of March. I was over on Main Street, looking up at the sign of a second floor nightclub called Florian's. There was a man near me looking up at the sign too, his eyes dreamy and a little shiny with tears, as if he was thinking of other people, other times he'd known there. He was a big man, but not much taller than six and a half feet and not much wider than a bus. His hands hung at his sides; in one of them was a forgotten cigar, smoking between his enormous fingers.

Passers-by were looking at him. He was interesting to look at, too, with his old gangster hat, worn, wool jacket with little white footballs on it for buttons, a brown shirt, yellow tie, grey trousers and snakeskin shoes with white bits over the toes. A bright yellow handkerchief, the same colour as his tie, was stuck in the top pocket of his jacket. Main Street isn't the quietest dressed street in the world, but even there you couldn't miss him. He was like a spider on a bowl of pink ice-cream.

He stood completely still, then slowly smiled and moved towards the door at the bottom of the steps up to the club. He went in and the door closed behind him. A couple of seconds later, it burst open again, outwards. Something flew out fast and landed between two cars on the street. A young black man in a purple suit with a little white flower in his buttonhole, stood up slowly, making a sad sound like a lonely cat, shook himself and walked painfully away down the street.

Silence. Traffic started again. It was none of my business at all, so I walked over to the door to take a look inside. A hand as big as an armchair, reached out of the darkness of the door and took hold of my shoulder, squeezing hard. The hand picked me up

1

and pulled me in through the door, up a step or two. A large face looked at me and a quiet voice said: 'Blacks in here now, huh? Just threw one out. You see me throw him out?'

He let go of my shoulder. It wasn't broken but I couldn't feel my arm. I kept quiet; there was talking and laughter from upstairs. The voice went on quietly and angrily: 'Velma used to work here. My little Velma. Haven't seen her for eight years. And now this is a black place, huh?' He took hold of my shoulder again, wanting an answer.

I said yes, it was, but my voice sounded broken and weak. He lifted me up a few more steps and I tried to shake myself free. I wasn't wearing a gun, but the big man could probably just take it away from me and eat it, so it wouldn't have helped.

'Go up and see,' I said, trying to keep the pain out of my voice.

He let go of me again, and looked at me with his sad, grey eyes. 'Yeah. Good idea. Let's you and me go on up and have a drink or two.'

'They won't serve you. I told you it's for blacks only up there,' I said, but he didn't seem to hear me.

'Haven't seen Velma in eight years. Eight long years since we said goodbye, and she hasn't written for six. Don't know why. She used to work here. Let's go on up now, huh?'

So we went up the stairs to the club. He let me walk, but my shoulder still hurt and the back of my neck was wet.

◆

The talking and laughter stopped dead when we walked in. The silence was cold and heavy, like a stone. Eyes looked at us, heads turned. A big, thick-necked black, with a flattened face, slowly stood up straight near the bar, getting ready to throw us out. He came towards us. My big friend waited for him silently and

2

didn't move when the black put his hand on the front of my friend's brown shirt and said: 'No whites in here, brother. Sorry. This place's for blacks only.'

'Where's Velma?' That's all he said.

The big black man nearly laughed. 'Velma? No Velma here, white boy. She's not in the business any more, maybe.'

'Velma used to work here,' the big man said. He spoke as if he was dreaming. 'And take your dirty hand off my shirt.'

That annoyed the black. People didn't speak like that to him, not in his job, throwing drunks out of the club. He took his hand off the shirt and then suddenly pulled back his arm and hit the big man hard on the side of the face. He was very good at hitting people hard, but this time it was a mistake. The big man didn't even move. He just stood there. Then he shook himself and took the black man by the throat. He picked him up with one hand, turned him in the air, put his other enormous hand against the black man's back and threw him right across the room. He went over a table and landed with a crash against the wall. The whole room shook. The black man didn't move – he just lay there in the corner.

The big man turned to me. 'Some guys,' he said, 'are stupid. Now let's get that drink.'

We went over to the bar. In ones and twos, like shadows, the other customers were moving towards the door, getting out of there fast.

'Beer,' the big man said to the white-eyed barman. 'What's yours?'

'Beer,' I said. We had beers. I turned and looked at the room. It was empty now, except for the big black man moving painfully out of the corner on his hands and knees, suddenly old and out of a job. The big man turned and looked too, but didn't seem to see him.

'You know where my Velma is?' he asked the barman.

'No whites in here, brother. Sorry. This place's for blacks only.'

'Beautiful redhead, she was. Sometimes sang here, too. We were going to get married when they sent me away.'

'Sent you away?' I asked. Stupid question.

'Where d'you think I've been these last eight years?' He looked quite pleased with himself. 'Prison. Malloy's my name. Moose Malloy. The Great Bend bank job – that was me. On my own, too. Forty thousand dollars.'

'You spending it now?' I asked, just trying to be polite.

He looked at me sharply. I was lucky – just at that moment, there was a noise behind us. It was the big, hurt black man going through another door at the other end of the room.

'Where does that door go to?' Moose Malloy asked the frightened barman.

'Boss's office, sir.'

'Maybe the boss knows where my little Velma is,' said Malloy, and crossed the room to the door. It was locked but he shook it open with one hand, went through and shut it behind him. There was silence for a minute or two. I drank my beer and the barman watched me.

Then suddenly, there was a short, hard sound from behind the door. The barman froze, mouth open, eyes white in the dark. I started moving towards the door, but it opened with a bang before I got there. Moose Malloy came through and stopped dead, a strange smile on his face. He was holding a gun.

He came across to the bar. 'Your boss didn't know where Velma is either. Tried to tell me – with this.' He waved the gun at us wildly. Then he started towards the door and we heard his steps going down fast to the street.

I went through the other door, to the boss's office. The big black man wasn't there any more, but the boss was. He was in a tall chair behind a desk, with his head bent right back over the back of the chair and his nose pointing up at the ceiling. His neck was broken. It had been a bad idea to pull that gun out when he was talking to Moose Malloy. There was a telephone on the desk, so I called the police. By the time they arrived, the barman had gone and I had the whole place to myself.

Chapter 2   The Right Kind of Bottle

A detective named Nulty took the investigation. I went with him to the 77th Street police station and we talked in a small, uncomfortable room which smelled of cheap cigars. Nulty's shirt was old and his jacket was worn. He looked poor enough to be honest, but he didn't look as if he'd be able to face Moose Malloy and win.

He picked up my business card from the table and read it.

'Philip Marlowe, Private Investigator. One of those guys, huh? So what were you doing while this Moose Malloy was breaking the black guy's neck?'

'I was in the bar. And he hadn't promised me he was going to break anybody's neck.'

'OK, funny guy. Just tell me the story straight.' Nulty didn't like my jokes.

So I told him about Moose Malloy: the size of the man, what he was wearing, why he was there and what happened in that nightclub bar. 'But I don't think he went in there to kill any-body,' I finished. 'Not dressed like that. He just went there to try to find his girl, this Velma who used to work at Florian's when it was still a white place.'

The phone rang on his desk. He picked it up and listened, wrote something on a piece of paper and put it down again.

'That was Information. They've got all the details on Malloy, and a photo.'

'I think you should start looking for the girl. Malloy's going to

6

be looking for her, so if you find her, you'll find him. Try Velma, Nulty, that's my advice.'

'You try her,' he said.

I laughed and started for the door.

'Hey, wait a minute, Marlowe.' I stopped and looked back at him. 'I mean, if you're not too busy, maybe you've got time to have a look for the girl. I'd remember your help, too. You PI's always need a friend down here among us boys, and I wouldn't forget it. Not ever.'

It was true. I wasn't at all busy. I hadn't had any real business for about a month. Even this job would make a change from doing nothing. No money in it, but a friend inside the police station might be useful one day.

That's how, when I'd eaten some lunch and bought a bottle of good whisky, I found myself driving north again on Main Street, following an idea that was playing around in my head.

♦

Florian's was closed, of course. I parked round the corner and went into a small hotel that was on the opposite side of the street from the club. A man with a very old tie, pinned in the middle with a large green stone, was sleeping peacefully behind the desk. He opened one eye and saw the bottle of good whisky standing on the counter right in front of his nose. He was suddenly awake. He studied the bottle carefully and he studied me. He looked satisfied.

'You want information, brother, you've come to the right place with the right kind of bottle.' He took two small glasses out from under his desk, filled them both and drank one straight down.

'Yes, sir. Certainly is the correct bottle.' He refilled his glass. 'Now, how can I be of help to you, brother? There's not a hole in the road round here that I don't know by its first name.'

7

I told him what had happened at Florian's that morning. He looked at me without much surprise and just shook his head.

'What happened to the guy who owned Florian's about six or eight years ago?' I asked him.

'Mike Florian? Dead, brother. Went to meet Our Maker five, maybe six years ago. Drank a bit too much, they said. Left a wife named Jessie.'

'What happened to her?'

'Don't rightly know, brother. Try the phone book.'

Clever guy, that. Why hadn't I thought of the phone book? He pushed the book across the desk to me and I looked. There was a Jessie Florian who lived at 1644 West 54th Place. I wrote down the address, shook hands with the man behind the desk, put the bottle back in the pocket of my jacket and went out to my car. Finding Malloy looked so easy now. Too easy.

Chapter 3 'Always Yours'

1644 West 54th Place was a dry-looking brown house with some dry-looking brown grass in front of it. Some half- washed clothes hung stiffly on a line to one side of the house. The bell didn't work so I knocked. A fat woman with a red face came to the door, blowing her nose. Her hair was grey and lifeless.

'Mrs Jessie Florian? Wife of Mike Florian?' I asked.

Her eyes opened in surprise. 'Why?' she asked. 'Mike's been dead five years now. Who d'you say you were?'

'I'm a detective,' I said. 'I'd like some information.'

She stared at me for a long minute, then pulled the door open and turned back into the house. The front room was untidy and dirty. The only good piece of furniture was a handsome radio, playing dance music quietly in one corner. It looked new.

The woman sat down and I did too. I sat on an empty whisky

'Mrs Jessie Florian? Wife of Mike Florian?'

bottle in the back corner of the chair. I wasn't too comfortable sitting on an empty bottle, so I pulled it out and put it on the floor by my chair.

'I'm trying to find a redhead, used to work at your husband's place over on Main Street,' I said. 'Singer, named Velma. I don't know her last name. I thought you might be able to help me.'

I brought out my nearly-full bottle of whisky and put it on the arm of my chair. Her eyes fixed immediately on the bottle in a greedy stare. I was right – a little whisky was going to help me again here. She got up, went out to the kitchen and came back with two dirty glasses. I poured her enough whisky to make her fly. She took it hungrily and put it down her throat like medicine. I poured her another. Her eyes were brighter already.

'Man, this stuff dies painlessly with me,' she said. 'Now, let me

9

think. A redhead, you say? Yeah. Maybe I can help you. I've got an idea.'

She got up with some difficulty and went out towards the back part of the house. The radio went on playing a love song to me. There were crashing noises from the room at the back – a chair had fallen over. I got up and walked quietly over. I looked round the edge of the open door. She was standing in front of a large open box, full of old books and pictures and envelopes. She took one envelope, fatter than the others, and quickly hid it down one side of the box. Then she picked up some others, shut the box and started back to the front room. I was sitting listening to the music by the time she got there.

She gave me a bright smile and handed me the old envelopes. Then she took the whisky bottle and went back to nurse it in her chair. I opened the envelopes one by one and looked through the old, shiny black-and-white photographs of singers and dancers and old-time jokers that were in them. One or two of them might have had red hair; you couldn't tell from the photographs.

'Why am I looking at these?' I asked her. She was having some trouble pouring the whisky into the glass now.

'Looking for Velma, you said. Could be one of those girls.' She was playing games with me, laughing at me while she finished my whisky.

I stood up, walked across the room and into the back room where the box was. There was an angry shout behind me. I reached down the side of the box, pulled out the fatter envelope and went back into the front room. She was standing in the middle of the floor, her eyes angry and dangerous.

'Sit down,' I said. 'You aren't playing games with Moose Malloy now. It's not that easy this time.'

'Moose? What about Moose?' The name had frightened her.

'He's out of prison and looking for his girl . . . with a gun.

I took out an old picture of a pretty girl with hair that might have been red.

He's already killed one guy who didn't want to tell him where Velma is.'

She went white, lifted the bottle to her mouth and poured the rest of the whisky straight down her throat. A lovely old woman. I liked being with her.

I opened the envelope in my hand and took out an old picture of a pretty girl in a funny hat with hair that might have been red. It was signed 'Always yours – Velma Valento.'

I held it up in front of the old woman.

'Why hide it?' I asked. 'Why is it different from the others? Where is she?'

I put the photograph back into the envelope and put the envelope into my pocket.

'She's dead. She was a good girl, Velma was. But she's dead. Now get out of here. I'm old and I'm sick. Get out.'

She suddenly lifted the empty bottle and threw it at me. It went off into a corner and banged against a wall. Then she sat down in her chair, closed her eyes and went to sleep. The radio was still playing in the corner. I went out to my car and drove back to the 77th Street police station, to Nulty's smelly little office.

♦

Nulty was sitting there looking at a police photograph of Moose Malloy. I told him about my visit to the hotel on Main Street and to Mrs Florian with my bottle of whisky. I told him about the dirty house and the new sixty-dollar radio in the front room there. And I showed him the photograph of Velma Valento.

'Nice,' he said. 'But what's happened to her?'

'Dead. That's what the Florian woman said. But then why did she hide the photo? I think she's afraid of Moose. I think she's afraid that Moose thinks she's the person who told the police about his bank job and got him put away in prison for eight years. Somebody told them. Maybe he knows who it was. Maybe he wants to find that person. But it's your job to find out what's happening here,' I said. 'I'm going home.'

'Hey! You aren't leaving me in this mess, are you?' he asked. 'What's the hurry?'

'No hurry at all,' I said, 'but there's nothing more I can do.' I walked to the door and out. Nulty didn't even say goodbye.

Chapter 4   Purissima Canyon

I was back in my office at about four-thirty when the phone rang. A cool voice said 'Philip Marlowe? The private detective?'

12

I said yes, maybe. The voice introduced itself: 'My name's Lindsay Marriott. I live at 4212 Cabrillo Street. I'd be very happy if you could come and discuss something with me this evening.'

'I'll be there,' I said. I needed a job. 'What time?'

He said seven, so I watched the sunlight dancing on my desk until almost seven, had a word or two with Nulty on the phone when he rang to see if I had any new ideas – I hadn't – and then I went out to Cabrillo Street. It was dark by the time I got there. Cabrillo Street was a dozen or so houses hanging onto the side of a mountain by the beach, with the Pacific Ocean crashing in below them. There were two hundred and eighty steps up from the street to Marriott's house, so I had to sit down for a few minutes at the top and try to start breathing quietly again before I knocked on the door.

It opened silently and I was looking at a tall man with fair hair, wearing a white suit with a blue flower in its buttonhole.

'Yes?' he said.

'It's exactly seven and here I am,' I answered.

'And you are . . . ?' He'd forgotten all about me.

'Philip Marlowe,' I said. 'Same as I was this afternoon.' I didn't think I liked this guy.

'Ah yes. Quite right.' He stepped back and said coldly 'Come in.'

The carpet was so thick it almost swallowed my shoes on the way through to the living-room, where Marriott arranged himself on a yellow sofa and lit a French cigarette. I lit a Camel and waited.

'I asked you to come because I have to pay some money to two men tonight and I thought I should have someone with me,' he said eventually. 'You carry a gun?'

'Sometimes,' I said. 'But I don't often shoot people. Blackmail, is it?'

13

I didn't like his smile. He was lying to me.

'Certainly not. I'm simply buying something and I'll be carrying a lot of money. Since I don't know these men, I thought . . .'

'But they know you, do they?'

'I – I don't know. I'm doing this for a friend, you see.'

'How much money – and what for?' I asked. I didn't like his smile. He was lying to me. 'Why don't you just tell me the whole story, Mr Marriott? If I'm going to hold your hand tonight, I think I should know why.'

He didn't like that, but in the end I got the full story. Three men had stolen a valuable diamond ring from his friend without a name a few nights before, when she was coming home from a restaurant in the city, and now they were selling it back for eight thousand dollars. He had spoken to one of the men on the phone two or three times, to help his friend, and now he was waiting for another call, to tell him where to meet them tonight with the money.

'So why did you only call me this afternoon, Mr Marriott? That worries me. And why did you choose me? Who told you about me?'

He laughed. 'No one told me about you. I picked your name from the phone book. And I only decided to take someone with me this afternoon – I hadn't thought of it before.'

'So what's the plan?' I asked. 'Do I hide in the back of the car? And what do I do if these guys pull out a gun and shoot you or knock you on the head, take your eight thousand and run? Nothing I could do would stop them. These guys are robbers, Marriott. They're hard. I think I should walk away from this job, Marriott. But I'm stupid, so I won't. I'll come with you, but I'll drive the car and I'll carry the money. And you do the hiding in the back of the car. OK?'

He shook his head and looked unhappy but in the end he

agreed. Then the phone rang. Marriott's face went white as he took the call. He listened. I could hear a voice talking at the other end, but I couldn't hear the words.

'Purissima Canyon? . . . I know it . . . Right.' He put the phone down. 'You ready, Marlowe? Let's go.'

I had never heard of Purissima Canyon, but Marriott said it was quite near and that we had to be there in twelve minutes. He gave me an envelope with all that money in it. I stuck it in my pocket and we left.

◆

Fog had come in from the ocean now, so I drove Marriott's big foreign car quite slowly. We found Purissima Canyon without difficulty. It was a quiet, lonely place in the hills behind the city. No houses, no lights. It was as dark as a midnight church. I stopped at the end of the dirt road and switched off the engine.

'Stay there,' I whispered to Marriott, hidden in the back of the car. 'Your friends may be waiting off the road here. I'll take a look.'

I got out and walked along a small path down the hill. I stopped suddenly and stood in the dark, listening. Not a sound. I turned to go back to the car. Still nothing.

'No one here,' I whispered into the back of the car. 'Could be a trick.'

He didn't answer. There was a quick movement just behind my head, and afterwards, I thought I may have heard the sound of the stick in the air before it hit my head. Maybe you always think that – afterwards.

◆

I opened my eyes and looked up at the stars. I was lying on my back. I felt sick. All I could hear was insects in the night. I stood up carefully. My hat was still on my head. I took it off and

16

felt underneath it – a bit soft and painful on one side, but still working well enough. Good old head, I'd had it a long time and I could still use it, well, a little at least. I turned to look for the car, but it was gone. The envelope with the eight thousand dollars was gone too.

I started to walk slowly back along the dark road. Suddenly, I saw the dark shape of the car in front of me, round a corner. It was silent, lightless, all the doors shut. I went up to it, lit a match and looked inside while the match was burning. Empty. No Marriott, no blood, no bodies, nothing. Suddenly, I heard the sound of a car's engine. I didn't jump more than three feet in the air. Lights cut through the darkness, coming down the road towards me. The lights stopped for a minute just round the next corner, then they came on down the road. I hid behind Marriott's car. The lights came on down the hill and stopped right in front of Marriott's car. There was a laugh, a girl's laugh, a strange sound in that place. Then a girl's voice said: 'All right. I can see your feet. Come out with your hands nice and empty. I've got a gun on your ankles.'

I came up slowly, hands up, and looked straight at the light shining in my face.

'OK, don't move. Who are you? Is that your car?' the voice asked, but she sounded a bit frightened, like me.'

'Why did you stop up the road there?' I asked.

'So you ask the questions, huh?' she said. 'Well, I was looking at a man.'

'Tall, with fair hair?'

'Not any more,' she said quietly. 'Might have had fair hair – once.'

I didn't say anything for a moment. Then I said: 'All right, let's go and look at him. I'm a private investigator. Marlowe's the name. Philip Marlowe. My card's in my wallet. Shall I get it out and show you?'

He wasn't pretty to look at.

'No. You just walk in front of me and we'll go and take a look at what's left of your friend.'

I turned away from the light and went on up the dusty road, round the corner. The girl with the gun was right behind me.

Chapter 5   'Don't Call Me Annie'

She shone her light on the body. His fair hair was dark with blood now and more of it ran from the corner of his mouth. He wasn't pretty to look at. I went through his pockets but there was nothing very interesting. Just coins and keys, a small knife, someone's business card, that sort of thing. I put the business card in my pocket – might be useful later. The girl watched.

'You shouldn't do that,' she said. Then: 'Somebody must have hated him, to do that to him.'

'Somebody, yeah, but it wasn't me. So who was it?'

'I didn't think it was you,' she replied.

'Could have been you, couldn't it? I don't know. What are you doing out here alone at this time of night? And what's your name?'

'My name's Riordan. Anne. And don't call me Annie. I just go out for a drive sometimes at night. I like these hills at night; they're peaceful. Well, usually they are. I saw a light down here and thought it was odd. So I came down to see.'

'You do take some chances, Miss Riordan. A young lady out in these hills alone at night, going down a dark valley to investigate.'

'I had a gun. And what happened to your head?' She was shining her light right at me now. 'You don't look too good, Mr Marlowe. I think I should get you out of here.'

'I'd be grateful if you'd drive me to my car. It's at Cabrillo

Street, near the beach. He lived there.' I pointed down at Marriott's body.

'Sure. But shouldn't someone stay with him? And shouldn't we call the police?' she asked.

'No,' I said. 'Not yet. I'd like time to think about this first.'

So we got into her little car and she drove me out of there. My head hurt.

We didn't talk. Then she said: 'You need a drink. Come back to my place and clean yourself up, have a drink and call the police from there. It's just over on West 25th, 819.'

'Thanks,' I said, 'but I should get back to my car.' I didn't want her mixed up in this thing.

So she drove me back to the bottom of the steps up to Marriott's house, where I had left my car. I got out, said thanks and gave her my card. Then, I went over to the West Los Angeles police station on my own, feeling cold and sick.

◆

It was an hour and a half later. They had taken Marriott's body away and I had told my story three times to a man named Randall. The back of my head was hurting. I sat there looking at the cigarette between my fingers and felt about eighty years old.

Randall said coldly: 'Your story sounds silly, Marlowe.'

We went through the whole thing again, detail by detail and Randall came up with some ideas about the murder which I didn't like. They weren't right – I told him. He didn't like that either, but in the end he let me go home. The fog had completely cleared now. I wanted a drink badly but the bars were all closed. I drove home fast.

◆

I got up at nine the next morning, drank three cups of black coffee and read the morning papers. There was a short piece

20

about Moose Malloy, but nothing about Lindsay Marriott. I was just leaving when the phone rang. It was Nulty and he sounded annoyed.

'Marlowe? What're you doing on Malloy?'

'Nothing. I've got a headache. You mean you haven't got him yet?'

He hung up without answering. I drove over to my office, opened the outside door and went in. Anne Riordan looked up from the magazine she was reading and smiled at me. In daylight, her hair was a rich red colour, she had grey eyes, a small cheeky nose and a wide mouth. She had a nice smile. It was a face I thought I would like. Pretty, but not beautiful.

I opened the inside door and she followed me through into my office, sat down and took one of my cigarettes.

'You probably didn't think you'd see me again so soon. How's your head?'

'I'll live.'

'Were the police nice to you?'

'Same as usual. I left you out of my story. Don't know why.'

'Because they might be nasty to me and because I might be useful to you. Do you want to know who Marriott's friend was – the lady who lost her valuable ring?'

I froze. I hadn't said anything to her about the ring Marriott was trying to get back for his friend.

'I didn't say anything about a ring last night,' I said slowly. 'So you'd better tell me what you know and how you know it.'

'My father was a police officer. He's dead now. But it was easy for me to find out that Randall is investigating the Marriott murder and I went over to see him. He told me. Then I went over to the best jeweller's shop in town and asked the manager there. I told him I was a writer wanting to do a piece about famous and expensive diamonds. He told me the name of that diamond and who it belongs to. Easy, you see. It belongs to a very rich lady in Bay City, a Mrs Grayle. She's much younger than her husband and is very beautiful – she sometimes runs around town with other men, like Lindsay Marriott. I found out that last bit from a friend in one of the newspapers. He gave me a photo of Mrs Grayle, too. Look.'

She pushed a photograph of a young woman across my desk. I looked at it. Beautiful, about thirty years old – Mrs Grayle had it all.

'So I called Mrs Grayle and said I was your secretary. She'll see you this afternoon – she wants to get her diamond ring back, and she might want you to help her do that.'

'You have been busy, haven't you?' I said. She looked serious and hurt. Yes, I could certainly get to like that face a lot, I thought. I smiled at her. 'Listen, Anne. Killing Marriott was a stupid mistake. I don't think this gang meant to murder him at all. They wanted the money for the ring, that's all, and I guess it's all right if I try to help Mrs Grayle get the ring back, now that the gang have got their money for it.'

She nodded. 'You're wonderful,' she said softly, 'but you're crazy.'

The word hung in the air as she got up, went very quickly to the door and out.

I sat and thought about things. Then I took out that business card I had taken from Marriott's pocket last night and looked at it. Plain and expensive-looking, with the name 'Jules Amthor' on it, and under that, the word 'Psychiatrist'. No address. Just a Stillwood Heights phone number. There was something about Mr Amthor and his card, found in a dead man's pocket, that wasn't quite right. Could be interesting, I thought, so I picked up the phone and tried the Stillwood Heights number.

'You have been busy, haven't you?' I said. She looked
serious and hurt.

Chapter 6   A Glass of Something Golden

A woman's voice answered, dry and foreign-sounding. No, she said I couldn't speak to Mr Amthor, but she could take a message and maybe Amthor could see me next week. I spelled out my name, address and phone number for her and then said I wanted to see Amthor about Lindsay Marriott. I spelled that for her too. I said I wanted to see her boss soon – s-o-o-n. Fast. She understood. I hung up and poured myself a drink from the office bottle. Ten minutes later, she called back and said Amthor would see me at six that evening, that he'd send a car to fetch me.

I was half-way to the lift, on my way to get some lunch, when an idea hit me. I stopped and pushed my hat back on my head before going back into the office and calling a man I knew. I wanted to find out who owned old Jessie Florian's house on West 54th Place. He could help me. He called me back about three minutes later with the answer.

'Man named Lindsay Marriott,' he said. I think I thanked him, put the phone down and sat staring at the wall for a couple of minutes. Then I went down to the coffee shop, ate lunch, got my car out of the car-park and drove east again, to West 54th Place. I didn't have a bottle with me this time.

◆

I went first to the house next door where an old woman lived and watched everything in the street from her windows. She would have some answers. I asked her if a big man had been into Mrs Florian's house the day before, and she described Moose Malloy to me exactly. She also said Mrs Florian always received a letter by special delivery on the first day of every month. Tomorrow was the first of April – April Fool's Day.* I asked her

* *April Fool's Day*: a day when people play tricks on their friends and family.

24

to be sure to notice if the special letter came as usual, thanked her and walked across to the house next door.

No one answered when I knocked and rang. I tried again. No answer. The door was open, so I went inside. The radio was turned off but Mrs Florian was there, in the bedroom, in bed. She opened her eyes slowly and looked at me.

'Good afternoon, Mrs Florian,' I said. 'Are you sick?'

'You get him?' she answered.

'Who? The Moose? No, not yet, but we will. Why? You frightened of him?' No answer to that. I put a Camel in my mouth and waited.

'One thing,' I said after a minute or two, 'I found out who owns this house. Lindsay Marriott.'

Her body went stiff under the bedclothes, like wood. Her eyes froze. Suddenly, she threw back the covers and sat up with her eyes flaming and pointed a little gun at me. But I was too quick for her; I stepped backwards through the door and out.

'Think about it, Mrs Florian,' I shouted back over my shoulder. I went out of the house fast, but nothing happened. She probably couldn't walk straight enough to follow me and shoot me in the back. I drove away.

♦

I went to see Nulty at the 77th Street police station.

'You,' he said as I came in the door. 'I thought you weren't helping me with the Malloy investigation any more.'

'You still got that picture of Velma Valento? It's really mine and I'd like to keep it,' I said.

He found it under some papers and gave it to me. I put it in my pocket and left Nulty looking hopeless and helpless behind his desk.

The phone was ringing as I walked back into my office. It was the rich and beautiful Mrs Grayle, Marriott's friend who had lost

25

her diamond ring so carelessly, and she wanted to see me as soon as possible. She gave me her address: Aster Drive, Bay City. I was there almost before she had said goodbye.

◆

Aster Drive was full of nice big houses near the ocean. The man at the gate of the Grayles' place was ugly and unfriendly, but he let me in eventually and I parked next to the five or six cars in the driveway. The house itself wasn't much. Smaller than Buckingham Palace.* I rang the doorbell. A manservant opened it and showed me into a large expensive room. The three people in there stopped talking when I came in. One of them was Anne Riordan, holding a glass of something golden in one hand. Another was an older man with a sad face and the third was Mrs Grayle. She was better than her photograph – perfect, a dream, in fact. And she was giving me an interesting smile.

'Nice of you to come, Mr Marlowe,' she said. 'This is my husband.'

I shook hands with Mr Grayle and smiled at Anne Riordan, wondering what she was doing there. Mr Grayle poured me a whisky and then left. Anne Riordan said she had to be going too. She left too, without another look at me.

'Do you think you can help me?' Mrs Grayle asked. 'I'd be so happy if you could help. I was so shocked to hear about Lin Marriott. Poor Lin.'

'Who knew the true value of that diamond ring?' I asked. 'Did he?'

'I've wondered about that,' she replied, her face getting a hard look on it. 'He was with me that night, so he knew I was wearing the diamond on my hand all evening.'

'And what happened out there? How did these guys take it off you?'

* *Buckingham Palace*: the London palace of the king or queen of England.

'Nice of you to come, Mr Marlowe,' she said.

'They must have followed us from the Trocadero, where we had dinner. Lin was driving. We were in a dark street when suddenly a car passed us fast and just hit the side of our car, then stopped in front of us. A tall, thin man in a coat, with his hat low over his face, got out and pulled a gun on us. Another man came up on the other side of our car and took my jewellery and my handbag. They gave my bag back after going through it. Then they left and we went home. The next day I got a call from one of them and Lin agreed to talk to them for me. I think you know the rest of it.'

'Yeah. All except the blackmail. Marriott was a blackmailer, wasn't he? He was blackmailing you, wasn't he? You don't have to tell me why.'

She stopped to think. 'Yes, he was,' she said slowly. 'He lived from blackmailing rich women, like me.'

I had some of the story, but she wanted to meet me later that evening at a club in town. There was more to tell me.

♦

I drove out of the gate, waving to the ugly man there, and stopped just outside when I saw Anne Riordan's car standing at the side of the street. She gave me a nice smile.

'Who told you Marriott played his lady-friends for money?' I asked her.

'Just a guess,' she said. 'You probably want me to stay out of this business, don't you? But I thought I was helping a little. Sorry if I wasn't. It was nice to know you anyway.'

And she started her car and drove away fast down the street. I watched her go.

It was nearly six when I reached my office again. I lit a cigarette and sat down to wait.

Chapter 7   The House on the Hill

The man smelled. I could smell him from the other side of my office when he came in. Mr Jules Amthor's driver. He gave me one of Mr Amthor's cards, but I had seen one before – in a more interesting place. He also gave me a hundred dollars, from Mr Amthor. That was interesting.

I locked the office and the man drove me over to Stillwood Heights, getting green lights all the way. Some guys are lucky like that.

We drove up a long driveway with bright red flowers down the sides and stopped in front of a large lonely house right on top of the hill. The man opened the door for me and I got out. He led me into the house, into a lift where his smell was even worse than before, and up. There was a desk with a woman behind it when we stopped and the doors opened. She was the owner of the voice on the telephone. I gave her the hundred dollars.

'Sorry, it was a nice thought but I can't take this. I have to know what the job is before I take any money for it.'

She nodded, stood up and pressed a button on the wall. A hidden door opened noiselessly and closed again after I had gone through it without her. There was nobody in the dark room I was now in. I stood for thirty seconds wondering if someone was watching me.

Then another door opened quietly on the other side of the room, and a tall, thin, straight man in a black suit walked in quickly and sat down on a chair by a table in the middle of the room.

'How can I help you?' he asked. His eyes, deep and very black, seemed to look at me without seeing me, without feeling anything.

'You seem to forget why I came,' I said. 'By the way, I gave that hundred dollars back to your secretary. I wanted to know why your card was found in the pocket of a dead man last night.'

His face didn't change. 'There are things I do not know,' he said after a second or two, 'and this is one of them. Anybody can take one of my cards.'

I almost believed him. Almost, but not quite. 'Then why did you send me a hundred dollars?' I asked.

'My dear Mr Marlowe,' he said coldly, 'I am not a fool. I am in a difficult business, always in danger from doctors who do not believe in my work as a psychiatrist. I like to know why people are asking questions about me.'

So I told him the whole story of my meeting with Marriott and about Marriott's murder. Nothing changed in his face.

Then I had another idea. I asked: 'Do you know a Mrs Grayle too, by any chance?'

He did. She had seen him about some problem once. That's what I liked about this job – everyone knew everyone. Marriott, Grayle and now Amthor. I was sitting there feeling pleased with myself when suddenly all the lights went out. The room was as dark as death.

I kicked my chair back and stood up, but it was no good. I was too slow. I smelled the man behind me just before he took me by the throat and lifted me into the air. I stopped breathing. The only good thing about that was that I couldn't smell him any more.

A voice said softly: 'Let him breathe – a little.'

The fingers round my throat loosened and I fought my way free from them just in time for something hard to hit me on the mouth. I tasted blood. The voice said: 'Get him on his feet. Stupid man. I think he can stand on his own now.'

The lights went on again and the arms dropped away. I stood, shaking my head, trying to think straight. Then I went for the smile on Amthor's face with everything I had in my right arm. It wasn't too bad. I hit the smile straight in the middle. Amthor looked surprised, very angry, and hurt. Suddenly there was a gun in his hand.

'Sit down, fool,' he said, pointing it at me. Blood was coming out of his nose. I sat down near the table.

Suddenly, everything in my head went black. Maybe I went to sleep just like that, with the nasty thin man in the black suit pointing his gun at me. I wasn't too sure when I thought about it later.

♦

When I woke up, I was in a small room with white walls and no window. My throat felt as if someone had jumped on it and I couldn't see clearly. It was as if there was smoke in front of my eyes, filling the room. I was in a bed. I began to remember things: Amthor and the man who smelled, breaking Amthor's nose. That made me feel better. But then they must have given me some sort of drug to knock me out, or to make me talk, and now I was having a hard time coming out of it.

I sat up on the bed and put my feet on the floor. I started to walk across the little room. It wasn't easy. It was as if I had drunk too much. But slowly the smoke started to clear from in front of my eyes. I walked and walked and walked round the room, with my knees shaking but my head getting clearer all the time.

There was a bottle of whisky on a small table in one corner but it smelled funny, more drugs in it maybe, so I didn't take a drink. But I could use it another way. I picked it up, went over to the door and shouted 'Fire! Fire!' Steps came running, a key was pushed into the lock and the door jumped open. I was flat against the wall to one side and I hit him with the bottle as he came in – a small, square, strong man in a white coat. Another friendly psychiatrist, maybe. He was out cold on the floor, with funny-smelling whisky and pieces of broken bottle all over him. I went through his pockets and took his keys, then I tied him to the bed

31

'Sit down, fool,' he said, pointing his gun at me.

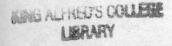

with his white coat. One of his keys opened the cupboard in the corner of the room and all my clothes were in there. So was my gun, but someone had kindly taken all the bullets out of it.

I locked the man in the room and went quietly across the carpet, listening to the silence of the house and holding the empty gun in front of me. There was an open door, with a light on in the room, just in front of me. I heard a man cough. Very carefully I looked into the room. He was reading a newspaper. I could only see the side of his face – he needed a shave. But Mr Moose Malloy was having a nice comfortable time hiding in this place, wherever it was. It was time for me to get out, though, to go far away, fast, so I left him there and moved quietly on.

♦

I walked on quietly through the empty house, past rooms with white walls and medicine bottles and metal tables with instruments on them. I saw a clock which told me it was almost midnight but I didn't meet any of the lovely people who worked in the place. At last, I came to the front door. It wasn't locked. I walked out into the night.

It was a cool night, no moon. The house was on the corner of a street. The sign said Descanso Street. I started to walk as fast as I could, listening for the scream of police cars coming to take me back there, but nothing happened.

I knew I was somewhere near the address Anne Riordan had told me for her apartment, at 819 25th Street. I worked my way across the streets towards it, and then realized I was still holding my gun in my hand. I put it away fast and kept on walking. The fresh air helped; I started to feel a bit better.

The light was still on at number 819, so I rang the bell. A voice from behind the door said: 'Who is it?'

'Marlowe.'

'My God!' she cried. 'You look like a ghost.'

The door opened and Anne Riordan stood there looking at me. Her eyes went wide and frightened.

'My God!' she cried. 'You look like a ghost.'

Chapter 8   Brains Behind the Business

I was half-sitting and half-lying in a deep chair in her comfortable living-room with its pleasant furniture and curtains. Anne sat opposite, her eyes dark and full of worry. She had made me three cups of black coffee and two eggs with some toast and I had told her some of the story, but not all of it. I had not told her the bit about Moose Malloy.

'Amthor's a nasty, hard guy,' I said. 'But I don't think he's clever enough to be the brains of a jewel gang. Perhaps I'm wrong, but my guess is that I wouldn't have got out of his little hospital if he was boss of a gang like that. I'd be dead.'

'But he's frightened of something, isn't he? He doesn't like the questions you're asking.'

I nodded. 'I think Marriott carried Amthor's card in his pocket that night exactly because he wanted it to be found if anything happened to him. So we know that the jewel robbery had something to do with Marriott's murder and I'm beginning to think Amthor had something to do with the jewel robbery. But I don't think he's the top man.'

Her smile was warm but as sharp as a razor at the same time. 'I forgot you were such a great detective. You get blood all over your face, you get yourself locked up in a hospital for two days, shot full of drugs, and after all that you arrive at the most obvious answer. Wonderful!'

I stood up. 'Yeah. I'm a little slow and tired tonight. Would you be kind enough to drive me to a taxi stand? I need a good night's sleep so that I can think out a better answer. And I don't want to stay anywhere too near those guys in that hospital. People round there don't seem to like me too much.'

She went quiet. 'You could stay here and . . .'

'You promise you'll lock your door?'

She went red and stood up. 'Sometimes I think you're the greatest thing I've ever seen and sometimes I think you're the worst, the lowest – you're sick.'

She walked out of the room fast and came back with her coat on, her red hair looking as angry as her face. She drove me all the way home, silent and angry, and when she dropped me at the door of my apartment she said goodbye in a frozen voice. She drove away before I had my keys out of my pocket.

♦

In the morning, I felt a lot better. My head still hurt and my tongue still felt dry and sticky inside my mouth, but I had known worse mornings. My left foot felt fine. It didn't hurt at all. So I kicked the corner of the bed with it on my way to the bathroom. I was just calling myself some very rude names when there was a loud knock on the door.

Police Detective Randall stood there – brown suit, hat, very clean and tidy, and a nasty look in his eye. He pushed the door and I stood back. He came in and looked around.

'Where've you been, Marlowe? Wanted to talk to you.'

'I've been sick. In a hospital.' I lit a cigarette. 'And I haven't had my morning coffee yet. I'm not feeling too friendly.'

'I thought I told you to keep out of this investigation, leave it alone, didn't I? I could make trouble for you, but I haven't. You know why?'

'Yeah. You couldn't find me.'

Very slowly he took a packet of cigarettes from his pocket, trying to control himself. His hand was shaking when he lit his match. I went out to the kitchen to make some coffee. He didn't like that either but he followed me out.

'This jewel gang has been around Hollywood for the last ten years,' he said. 'This time they went too far. Killed a man. I think I know why.'

I got the cream from the refrigerator, poured two cups of coffee and we sat down.

'Was that a joke about being in hospital?' he asked.

'No. I ran into some trouble over at Stillwood Heights and some kind people put me in a hospital just over the line, in Bay City. Place for drink and drugs problems. Nice little place. Shot me full of drugs and kept me there for two days until I woke up and walked out to see a friend.'

'Bay City?' he said. 'Man named Jules Amthor? Why did you take that card, Marlowe? You should have told me about it. You see, your friend over in Bay City, the redhead, she told me. She likes you. She was hoping to help you out of a tight corner with me. Her father was a police officer, remember.'

'Ah, hell! Trying to help me. Nice girl. Not my type, though.'

He smiled his first smile of the day. He probably only let himself have four smiles a day. I could see he didn't believe me, so I went on: 'This is what I think, if it's any use to you, Randall. I think Marriott was a blackmailer of rich women. Mrs Grayle told me so. But I think he was also the finger man for the jewel gang, the boy who could point them in the right direction, tell them where the really expensive pieces were and exactly when and where to move in on his lady- friends when he took them out to dinner. You see, in this Grayle robbery, Marriott had taken Mrs Grayle to the Trocadero and he was driving the car on their way home. He could choose the streets they took and the gang could follow. I think they killed Marriott because people were starting to put two and two together about him, and the answer was four. He wasn't useful to them any more, so this was his last job for them. But Marriott guessed something was going wrong and got frightened. He asked me to go along with him and he had the little trick of Amthor's card in his pocket. He was trying to show us who the real brains behind the business were – a guy quite nasty enough and clever enough, and also a guy who could get information about rich women when they came to talk to him about their problems. A very friendly psychiatrist. And Marriott's trick with Amthor's card worked, too, didn't it?'

'I think your ideas about Marriott may be right,' he said. 'But you haven't told me the whole story, everything you know, have you, Marlowe? Marriott had twenty-three thousand dollars in the bank. That's a lot of money. But there's also the little matter of that nice house he owned up on West 54th Place. Number 1644. That interest you at all?' He picked up a spoon and started to turn it in his hand. I didn't answer; just looked at him. He went on: 'You see, I can put two and two together as well,

Marlowe. And that brings a large ex-prisoner called Moose Malloy into the picture, doesn't it?'

'I'm listening,' I said.

'So I called up Detective Nulty, who I hear is investigating that one, and he told me you were trying to find a girl called Velma something, Malloy's girl. He said you'd been to see a woman by the name of Jessie Florian. And her address was – guess where? – 1644 West 54th Place. The place Marriott owned. So here I am, early this sunny morning, asking you a few questions and you're not helping me much.'

I went over to my jacket, hanging on the back of a chair. I wondered if they'd taken my two photos out at the hospital place, but they were both still there: the one of Velma Valento from Mrs Florian's box and the one of Mrs Grayle, which Anne Riordan had given me. I gave the one of Velma to Randall first. He studied it carefully. Then I put the one of Mrs Grayle next to it.

He looked at it and nodded. 'For twenty million I'd marry her myself,' he said.

'There's another thing I ought to tell you,' I said. 'This hospital I was in, down on Descanso in Bay City. They're running a hiding place for gangsters there too. I saw Moose Malloy there last night. In a room.'

Randall sat very still, watching me. 'Sure?' he asked.

'I didn't make a mistake,' I said. 'Even though I was full of drugs. It was him all right.'

He stood up. 'Let's go and see this Mrs Florian together, you and me.'

I told him everything I knew about this business while we were on our way.

Chapter 9   The *Montecito*

The old woman in the house next door was still watching every-thing that moved in the street and her eyes were just as sharp as ever. She didn't have anything new to tell us so we walked across to the next house. The same washing was still hanging stiffly on the washing line at the side of the house. There was no answer when we rang the bell and none when we knocked at the door. The door was locked this time. We went round to the back door. That was locked too but Randall kicked it open and we walked past a row of empty whisky bottles in the kitchen, into the living-room. The place smelled horrible. The radio was off.

'Nice radio,' said Randall.

Mrs Florian was in the bedroom. She hadn't been dead for very long. Long enough to be completely dead, though. Randall looked at her.

'This was done the quiet way,' he said. 'Just one large pair of hands round her neck. Enormous hands. Look at the marks on her neck.'

'You look at them,' I said and turned away, feeling ill again.

◆

We went back to Randall's office at the police station, and Randall made me make a full report on the story I had told him in the car and on the murder we had found at West 54th Place. I signed four copies.

'Now let me tell you something, Marlowe,' he said, sitting back in his chair. 'Her neck was broken first and then the mur-derer started to hit her. Why did he hit her when she was already dead? Answer: he was angry with her. A thousand dollars was paid to the person who gave Malloy's name to the police after the Great Bend bank job eight years ago, and I think the Florians got some of that money. Malloy may have thought the same

39

She hadn't been dead for very long. Long enough to be completely dead, though.

thing. Maybe he was just trying to make her tell him who gave the police his name. It was Malloy who killed her all right, even if it was a mistake. Perhaps he's just too strong.'

'Perhaps,' I answered.

'Now here's some advice for you, Marlowe, from a friend.' He used another one of his four smiles for the day on me. 'Go home and forget this whole investigation completely. Leave it alone. If you don't, you'll find yourself deep in trouble you won't be able to climb out of. Understand?'

I said I understood. He looked at me for ten seconds, then he smiled again. He was doing a lot of smiling that day. Enough for a whole week.

I stood up and said goodbye, went home to get my car and ate some lunch in Hollywood before I drove over to Bay City. It was a beautiful afternoon, sunny but cool.

◆

I went to see the Chief of Police, a fat man named John Wax, who sat doing nothing in a big office marked 'Private'. I told him I was working for Mrs Grayle and that I was trying to find out more about Jules Amthor, the psychiatrist, and about the odd hospital for drink and drugs problems right there under his nose in Bay City. Could he help? It was the name Grayle which made him sit up straight in his chair. He asked me to go and lock the door, pulled out a bottle from somewhere in his desk and poured two drinks. He looked hurt as he drank his drink but in the end he agreed to help me in any way he could.

He sent a man down with me to look at the hospital on Descanso Street. It was a pleasant place by daylight, with a garden full of flowers of all sorts. It was quiet and still in the early afternoon sun. Outside, two men were studying a tall tree, as if they were wondering how to move it, and another was sitting in a car down the street reading a newspaper. My friendly Bay City policeman just drove straight past the house. He wasn't smiling.

'Los Angeles police. What the hell are they doing down here? This is our part of town, our side of the line. The Chief won't be pleased.'

He drove round the next corner and stopped.

'Who are the big guys in crime down here in Bay City?' I asked him. 'What kind of problems do you face down here?'

He didn't answer straight away. Then he said very quietly, so that I could only just hear: 'Man named Laird Brunette runs this town. Runs all the crime in Bay City. Owns those two gambling ships out in the ocean there, too, just beyond where we can reach them. We can't touch his gambling business or any other business out there . . .' He stopped. He'd said enough. His eyes started to worry that he'd said too much.

'Thanks,' I said and gave him my hand. He had given me my next idea.

◆

I found a hotel room down by the waterfront in Bay City and waited until it was dark. I could hear people talking together and cars passing along the street outside. I thought about the whole story of Malloy and Velma, Marriott and the beautiful Mrs Grayle, the attractive Miss Anne Riordan, the slow and stupid Nulty, the fat and lazy John Wax and the clever and deadly Detective Randall. I thought of psychiatrists and jewel gangs and hard men who took me by the throat and tried to stop me breathing. I thought about a lot of things. It got darker. I needed a drink, I needed a holiday in the sun, I needed a home in the country and I needed a friend, but all I had was a coat and a hat and a gun. I got up, washed my face and got ready for the night's work in front of me.

Outside, I walked slowly along the seafront and back again, watching the faces in the crowd and the lights of the two gambling ships out there on the dark ocean. A hamburger seller was shouting 'Get hungry, friends, get hungry! Nice fat hamburgers here. Get hungry!' I stopped and asked him the names of the two ships.

'*Montecito* and *Royal Crown*,' he said, looking at me with careful eyes. 'Why are you interested?'

I laughed and waited while he served a young couple with hamburgers. Then he came close and said quietly: 'You want to hide out there? It'd cost you a lot, friend. Not less than fifty to take you out there. The *Montecito* is the one you'd want.'

I left him wondering why I had asked him at all and walked further along the seafront, found a place to have dinner and sat down with a drink. The dinner tasted like a postman's sack and the waiter looked as if he'd cut my throat for a dollar. But the drink was good.

◆

I took a water-taxi out to the *Montecito* for a quarter of a dollar. It was a long way out over the dark sea. I stared at the orange lights of Bay City getting further and further away, disappearing now and then as the boat rode down between two waves. When we arrived, a dark-eyed young man in a blue jacket stepped in front of me as I went up the steps.

'Sorry, mister. No guns on the boat.'

'It's part of my clothes,' I told him. 'I'm here to see Mr Brunette on business.'

'Never heard of him,' he said, with a face like stone. 'Get back in the taxi and get on your way – fast. We're not in Bay City now. We're not even in California, so move.'

I got back in the boat. Blue Jacket watched me with a silent smile. The taximan didn't say a word the whole way back. As I got off at the waterfront, he handed me a quarter- dollar. 'Some other night, maybe,' he said in a tired voice.

There was a very big guy with red hair, dirty shoes and torn sailor's trousers in the crowd waiting for the next taxi. He didn't

'Get back in the taxi and get on your way — fast.'

fit in at all. As I went past him, he took my elbow. I stopped.

'What's the matter with you?' I asked. I wasn't feeling polite, even though he was three inches taller than me and heavier too.

'Couldn't get onto the ship?' he asked between his teeth. 'Trouble getting on with that gun under your coat, huh?' He looked up and down the waterfront. 'I can help, maybe. Can be done, you know. Fifty dollars.' I started to walk away but he kept hold of my elbow.

'OK. Twenty-five, for a friend.'

'I don't have any friends,' I said, and walked away. He didn't try to stop me. He followed me slowly along the waterfront, through the crowds. I stopped to watch some people playing bingo and he came up next to me – a handsome guy with blue eyes, as big as Moose Malloy but he looked younger and faster on his feet.

He said into my ear: 'What's your business? Private investigation? I was on the police here once. I can recognize guys like you.' He smiled.

'Know a man named Brunette, then?' I asked. The smile stayed on his face.

'I can borrow a very quiet boat, friend, and there's a place along there, with no lights, where we can leave and come in again without anyone seeing us.' He pointed along the waterfront with his chin. 'I know where there's a delivery door on the *Montecito* which you can open and get in, too.'

I got my wallet out and gave him twenty-five in new notes. He disappeared quietly among the crowd, with a smile. 'Give me ten minutes. My name's Red,' was all he said.

The noise of the bars and crowds died away behind me, and I found the nice dark place along the waterfront ten minutes later with no trouble. There were some steps down to the sea. I went down them as carefully as a cat and a big black shape suddenly appeared out of the darkness next to me. He pointed down to a

45

boat riding on the sea with its engine going almost noiselessly and said: 'OK. Get in.'

We moved out into the blackness of the sea and the waves again. It was not the happiest moment of my life. As we went out across the dark water, I told this big friendly giant why I was there, that I wanted to talk to a man called Laird Brunette, that I wanted to find an ex-prisoner and murderer called Moose Malloy who might be hiding out on the *Montecito*. I told him more than I meant to, but he listened and thought a bit and then said: 'Yeah. Brunette runs all the gambling, the drugs and the women in this town. Maybe he runs that hospital they put you in, too. But I just don't think Brunette would be behind that jewel robbery you were talking about. He's big time, and that's too small. I don't think he had anything to do with that. And I don't think Brunette would hide a man like Malloy,' he said, 'unless there's something other than money behind it which is worrying him.' He moved his hands on the wheel of the boat and said: 'I don't like these guys at all. I really hate them, in fact.'

So I had a friend. We moved quietly in towards the enormous black side of the *Montecito*. There were two big iron doors in the side of the ship, just higher than our little boat. We stopped near them and rode up and down on the waves, listening. Everything was quiet except the sound of water and the music up above us.

Chapter 10   'My Little Velma'

Red threw a rope up over the side of the *Montecito* and pulled himself up quietly to the two iron doors. There was a sound of metal over my head and then I started up the rope. It was the longest journey I've ever made. It finished inside the oily, bitter-smelling darkness of the ship with rats running across the boxes and ropes on the floor.

A voice next to my ear said quietly: 'From here we go straight up through the engine-room. There'll probably be one guy in there. Might have a gun, but that's no problem. Then I'll show you the way up to the gambling rooms. That's where you're going to find Brunette. I'll wait for you in the engine-room. You may need some help up there.'

'You got family on this ship or something?' I asked, but he was already in front of me, the rats running away from his enormous feet in the darkness. The man in the engine-room was no problem, as Red had promised. He hit him hard, once, and caught him as he fell. Then he showed me the stairs up to the music and the people.

'How long will you be?' he asked.

'Don't know. An hour or less, I guess. But don't wait for me. Get out now. I'm going to make some trouble on this ship.' And I went away up the steps.

He hit him hard, once, and caught him as he fell.

♦

I came out on an open walkway on the ocean side of the ship. There was a man with a small machine-gun in the shadows there. I went up behind him silently and put my gun in his back.

'I have a very loud gun,' I said. 'But it doesn't have to go off. All I want is to talk to Brunette. Now why don't you show me the way nice and peacefully?'

He took a moment or two to think about all that. Then he said: 'OK. Follow me across to that door. We're going down to the offices past the gambling tables.'

We went into the bright lights inside the ship and through the gambling rooms, where sixty or seventy people were trying not to lose their shirts. I put my gun away under my coat as we went.

Two quiet men in black dinner jackets came through a door on the other side of a bar and came towards us.

'People round here don't seem to follow their orders,' the short one said.

'You're Brunette,' I said suddenly.

'Of course.' He turned and opened a door behind him. 'In here. We can talk more easily.'

I followed him through into a comfortable small office with photographs on the tables and a small private bar in one corner. He sat down.

'He has a gun,' Brunette said.

A hand took the gun away from me and put it down on Brunette's desk.

'Anything more, boss?' a voice asked.

'Not now.' He turned to me and said: 'Who are you and what do you want?'

'My name's Marlowe. I'm a private detective and I want to talk to a man called Moose Malloy. I'm investigating a murder, the murder of a man named Marriott. That murder has something to do with another one – of an old woman – which was done by Malloy. Malloy was staying at a hospital for drug problems over in Bay City, hiding from the law, and now he's disappeared. I think he could be hiding here on your nice gambling boat.'

'You're simple,' Brunette said. 'Why should I hide gangsters here? I'm in another business. Sorry, but I can't do anything for you. But I'd like to know how you got onto my ship.'

'I just can't remember.'

'You do take some terrible chances, Mr Marlowe.' He smiled a nasty, cold smile.

'Just give this to Malloy first,' I said, and I reached across his desk, took a card and wrote five words on it. 'It'll mean something important to him.'

'OK,' he said. 'If I can get this to Malloy, I will. I don't know why I'm doing it for you.' He pushed my gun back across the desk to me and stood up. 'But I promise nothing, Marlowe.' He put out his hand and I shook it. I went back to Bay City the ordinary way, in a water-taxi. There was already a new man at the top of the steps – Blue Jacket was gone. I wondered if he was already dead or working down in the engine-room for letting me get onto his boss's ship with my gun.

Back on the waterfront I found Red.

'Get your man?' he asked.

'No. But I think Brunette will find a way to get a message to him for me. Could take hours; could take days. I might never find him – alive.'

♦

I drove back to my apartment in Hollywood and called the Grayle number. Mrs Grayle agreed to come over to my apartment and go out somewhere for a drink. Then I lay down on my bed and tried not to go to sleep. I failed, though. I could have slept for a week.

I woke up slowly and stared at the light of the lamp on the

ceiling. Something moved gently in the room. Moose Malloy, with a gun in his hand and his hat pushed back on his head. He saw me open my eyes.

'Glad you came over,' I said.

'Your door wasn't locked so I came on in. You waiting for visitors?'

'A lady. She may not come. But I'd prefer to talk to you.'

A smile touched the corners of his mouth.

'I'd like to talk about the killing of a woman. Jessie Florian. I think that was a bad mistake. You didn't mean to kill her; you just wanted her to tell you something. That's all, isn't it? You wanted her to tell you where Velma was, but she didn't even know. Velma was too clever for her.'

The smile had gone from his mouth. He kept quiet.

There was a knock on the door. I got up from the bed and went through to the living-room to open it. Malloy stayed in the bedroom, in the dark. She stood there half-smiling, beautiful, in a high-necked white evening dress with deep, red stones circling the creamy white of her neck. Her smile died when she saw me in my old work suit and her eyes went cold. I stood to one side and held the door open. She walked in past me and then turned quickly, annoyed.

'Have a drink,' I said. 'Then let's talk. Not about stolen diamond rings, but about murder.'

I went through to the kitchen and mixed some drinks, leaving her staring at my back. When I came back, she was sitting coolly in my best chair, blowing smoke from her cigarette up at the ceiling.

'Personally, I don't believe that Lindsay Marriott was the finger man for a jewel gang, though that's what the police seem to think,' I began. 'And I don't think he was a blackmailer either. Funny, isn't it, Mrs Grayle? And I don't think he was killed by any gang, or that he was going to Purissima Canyon that night to buy back a diamond ring for you. I don't think a diamond ring was ever stolen, in fact. I think he thought he was going there to help someone with a murder, but in fact he was going there to die. Someone wanted Lin Marriott dead.'

Her smile was like broken glass now. Suddenly she wasn't beautiful any more; she was wild and very dangerous. All she said was: 'And who did he think he was going to help murder, Mr Marlowe?'

'Me. Philip Marlowe. And I'll tell you why. Simply because I was trying to find a girl who used to sing at a nightclub over on Main Street, a place called Florian's. Her boyfriend was looking for her too – an ex-prisoner named Moose Malloy. Perhaps I was helping Malloy find this girl, and I was starting to ask all the wrong questions, so he was told I had to die.'

She nodded and said, 'Very interesting, if I knew what you were talking about.'

'And you do,' I said.

We stared at each other. She had her right hand inside her little white handbag now. I knew what she held in it but she wasn't ready yet. These things take time.

'Let's stop playing games, shall we, Mrs Grayle? A girl who came up the hard way eventually married a very, very rich man and went to live with him at his place near the ocean. Aster Drive. But one day, an old woman recognized her and this old woman started to blackmail our beautiful young lady. The old woman had to be kept quiet. Marriott helped his beautiful friend by paying some money to the old woman on the first of every month, special delivery, but he and the old woman were the only two people who knew the secret. Some day, the young woman's boyfriend was going to get out of prison and come looking for his girlfriend, and she didn't want him to find her. So when this private investigator started pushing his nose in and asking questions, Marriott had to die, even though he thought he was

51

'You sent me away for eight years. My little Velma.' She shot him
five times.

going to help murder me. He knew too much. He was the real danger, not me. So you killed him, didn't you, Mrs Grayle?'

Her gun came out then. She pointed it at me and smiled. I did nothing. But Moose Malloy stepped through the door of the bedroom with a larger gun in his hand. He didn't look at me at all. He spoke softly: 'Thought I knew the voice. I tried to remember that voice for eight years while I was away. I liked your hair better when it was red, though. Hello, baby.'

She turned the gun on him.

'Get away from me,' she said.

'And I just realized in there who it was that gave my name to the police after the Great Bend bank job. You. Little Velma. You sent me away for eight years. My little Velma.'

She shot him five times. He stayed standing, then he fell face down. She ran to the door and out. I didn't try to stop her. I turned Malloy over carefully and put a pillow under his head, but after five shots in the body even Moose Malloy wasn't going to live very long. Then I called Randall at his home and told him what had happened.

The police cars were there with a doctor a couple of minutes later and the doctor said he had a chance. I knew he wouldn't want it. He didn't. He died in the night.

◆

It took three months to find Velma. Randall told me the details. She was hiding in the most obvious place. One night, a detective with a good memory walked into a nightclub in New York and heard a singer he liked there. But something about her face made him go back and look at the 'Wanted' photographs on the wall of his office. She was there, all right, so he went back to the club and showed her her name and picture on the list. But he was too careless. She pulled a gun out of her bag when he was taking her in, and shot him three times. Then she used her last two bullets on herself. Velma was tired of running away.

ACTIVITIES

Chapters 1–2

Before you read

1 Philip Marlowe is a famous fictional detective. What other famous detectives from films or books can you think of? In your opinion, what qualities does a successful private detective need?

2 Find these words in your dictionary. They are all in the first two chapters:

bang   guy   investigation   whisky

   a All of these words are nouns. Which one can also be used as a verb?

   b Which word describes:
      (i) a drink? (ii) a detective's work? (iii) a man? (iv) a noise?

   c What adjective and verb can be made from *investigation?*

After you read

3 What do you know about these characters? Match the names on the left with the correct description on the right.

   a Philip Marlowe   is a poor policeman.
   b Moose Malloy   used to own a nightclub.
   c Jessie Florian   used to sing in a nightclub.
   d Mike Florian   breaks a man's neck.
   e Detective Nulty   isn't very busy.
   f Velma Valento   lost her husband six years ago.

4 Are these sentences true or false? Correct the false ones.

   a Moose Malloy has been in prison for eight years.
   b Velma sometimes visited Moose in prison.
   c Malloy had planned to kill the boss of the nightclub.
   d Marlowe agrees to look for Velma because he needs the money.
   e The man who works opposite the nightclub tells Marlowe where to find Jessie Florian.

Chapters 3–4

Before you read

5 What is *blackmail*? Check the word in your dictionary.
6 At the end of Chapter 2, Marlowe goes out to his car.
   Who is he going to visit, and why?

After you read

7 What is unusual about Jessie Florian's front room? Why do you
   think this interests Marlowe?
8 How does Jessie feel when Marlowe tells her that Moose is out of
   prison? Why?
9 On page 15, Lindsay Marriott says: 'Since I don't know these men,
   I thought . . .' but he doesn't finish the sentence. What do you think
   he is going to say before Marlowe interrupts him?
10 According to Marriott, why does he have to give these men
   $8,000?
11 How does Marlowe meet the girl with the gun? What does she
   want to show him?

Chapters 5–6

Before you read

12 What is a *psychiatrist*? Find the word in your dictionary.
   Practise the pronunciation.
13 Look at the picture on page 18. Who is the dead body? If you were
   Marlowe, what would you do now?

After you read

14 What is the connection between Lindsay Marriott and:
   a Mrs Grayle?
   b Moose Malloy?
   c Jules Amthor?
15 Work in pairs. Act out the conversation between Marlowe and
   Randall on page 20.

Student A: You are Randall. You have to solve Marriott's murder. Ask Marlowe to tell you everything he knows. You think that the story is silly, and that Marlowe is hiding something, so check his story carefully. Try to find out what information Marlowe is hiding from you.

Student B: You are Marlowe. Tell Randall the truth about what happened with you and Marriott, but don't say anything about Anne Riordan.

16 What information does Anne Riordan find out? How does she discover this?

17 Why does Mrs Grayle want to see Marlowe? What information does she try to hide from him?

Chapters 7–8

Before you read

18 At the end of Chapter 6, Marlowe sits down to wait.
What is he waiting for, do you think?

After you read

19 Why does Marlowe think that
  a Jules Amthor isn't the top man in the jewel gang?
  b Marriott carried Amthor's card in his pocket?
  c Marriott helped the gang to steal Mrs Grayle's diamond?
  d the gang killed Marriott?
  e Marriott asked him (Marlowe) to go with him to meet the gang at Purissima Canyon?
  f Jules Amthor is connected to the criminal world?

20 What *new* information does Detective Randall give Marlowe about Lindsay Marriott?

21 Detective Randall tells Marlowe that Anne Riordan likes him. What does Marlowe say about Anne? Do you believe him?

Chapters 9–10

Before you read

22 Find these words in your dictionary:

bingo   gambling   rope   waterfront

Which of these words would be important to

a a sailor?

b a mountain-climber?

c someone who enjoys games of luck?

d someone who wants to win a lot of money?

23 Look at the picture on page 40. Who is dead, do you think? Who are the two men, and what might they be thinking?

After you read

24 How are the following things important to the story?

a $1,000	**e** a white handbag
b The *Montecito*	**f** a pillow
c $25	**g** a photograph on a wall
d a card	

25 How are the following new characters important to the story?

a John Wax?

b Laird Brunette?

c Red?

26 Marlowe discovers a lot of secrets in the last chapter.

What secrets does he discover about

a Lindsay Marriott?

b Jessie Florian?

c Mrs Grayle?

27 What does Moose Malloy suddenly realize just before he dies?

28 At the end of the story, which of the criminals does Marlowe feel most sorry for, do you think? How does he show this? Do you agree with Marlowe?

Writing

29 You are Philip Marlowe. Write a report for the Bay City Police about these people. Who killed them, why, where and when?

a Lindsay Marriott

b Jessie Florian

c Moose Malloy

30 Read the first paragraph on page 1 again and lines 10–14 on page 53. Think about Moose Malloy's real feelings. Write *his* story. Begin like this: 'Eight years ago I . . .' Put his thoughts and feelings, as well as his actions, into the story.

31 You are Philip Marlowe. You haven't seen Anne Riordan since she drove you home (page 35). She was angry when she said goodbye to you. Write a letter to her, telling her what happened after you left her. Thank her for all the help she gave you, apologize for making her angry, and tell her that you would really like to see her again.

32 You are the Bay City Chief of Police, John Wax. You decide to bring in Laird Brunette and Jules Amthor. Write your reports on these two men. Talk about their criminal activity in general, and their importance in the Velma Valento/Moose Malloy case.

33 Many crimes are committed in this story: blackmail, murder, robbery, kidnap. Write about crime in your country. Which crimes are the most common, and which are the most serious? How are criminals punished for these crimes? Do you think that punishment in your country is too light or too heavy?

34 Red is having a drink with a friend in a waterfront bar, waiting for Marlowe to return from the *Montecito*. This is the beginning of their conversation:

Friend: What's the matter, Red? You look nervous tonight. What's the problem?

Red: I've had a really strange adventure tonight. You'll never believe me.

Friend: Tell me about it.

Write the rest of the conversation between them. Red tells his friend everything that has happened so far, what he hopes Marlowe is doing on the ship, and what he will do if Marlowe doesn't come back soon.